The Sinking

A Little Mermaid Retelling Novella

by

K M Robinson

THE SINKING
Copyright © 2018 by K.M. Robinson.

Published by Crescent Sea Publishing.
www.crescentseapublishing.com

Cover designed by Reading Transforms.
Image copyright © K.M. Robinson Photography.

This is a work of fiction. Names, characters, brands, trademarks, places, and incidents either are the product of the author's imagination or are used fictitiously. Any resemblance to actual events, locales, organizations, or persons, living or dead, is entirely coincidental and beyond the intent of either the author or the publisher.

*To my mother who inspired my love of mermaids from the time
I was little*

CHAPTER One

THE CHIMES JINGLE AS THE PAWNSHOP DOOR CLOSES. I probably shouldn't have sold them, but mother says I need to stop hoarding the merchandise.

The shop is usually quiet this time of day, the mothers all picking their children up from school, the men still at their jobs and unable to get off early and come trade two week's worth of pay for a ring for a pretty girl, and the old men that come looking to flirt are still at their late lunches.

I regret giving away the chimes instantly. They're made of metal bars and little seashells—I could easily make another—but I don't like giving my treasures away.

At least the older woman paid extra for it.

I walk away from the register, rifling through my bag on the floor. I look up as the door clicks opens—I was right, I shouldn't have sold the chimes.

Before I can straighten, a woman hovers in front of

me on the opposite side of the counter. She smiles a toothy grin at me.

"I'd like to trade this," she says, holding out a necklace.

I hold out my hand, allowing her to rest the shell in it. Lifting it up, I examine the golden detail work around the metallic shell. The bottom opens, revealing a storage space, though nothing resides inside the shell.

"Legend says, if you dip it into the sea and call out to the waves, it will turn you into a mermaid," she informs me. "If you find your love below the waves, you get to stay, but if you don't, you drown beneath the waves."

"Why are you pawning this?" I ask, closing the bottom of the necklace.

We're not required to ask why people part with their things, but I have nothing better to do while trapped in the tiny shop on the pier. She looks at me thoughtfully.

"My son is in need," she says. "I'll get it back if it doesn't work out."

"I can give you fifty dollars for this," I inform her after examining it—the gold alone is worth more.

"All right," she says, ducking her head. She quietly accepts the money form me.

I push the cash register closed as she heads toward the door.

"You have until the twenty-first to come back for this, ma'am," I call after her.

"Thank you, anemone," she calls back. "Feel free to

wear it until then—it would look beautiful on you. You can even try it in the water if you want to see a little magic."

She winks, turning back toward the door as she fans the ten-dollar bills out that I gave her.

"Try it on now," she insists, spinning back to me, nearly toppling the hair piled on her head under her wrap. "I'd love to see it on you."

I try to refuse but finally give in when she lingers in the doorway, waiting, a wrinkled hand on the doorframe. I clasp it around my neck, allowing her to see the gold piece rest on my collarbone.

As she exits, an older man walks in, looking for nothing in particular other than to spend a few minutes trying to make a pass at me. I show him a few things that recently became available but, inevitably, he turns them all down and leaves empty-handed.

By the time things slow down, the sun is setting over the horizon, casting marvelous colors out onto the ocean's surface. I lock the shop up for the night and wander down the pier.

Slipping my shoes off, I walk through the sand at the water's edge. One of the benefits of living near the ocean is walking in the waves every night after the tourists have gone home—that and perfect beach hair every single day.

I make it all the way to the next pier before I realize I left the necklace on accidentally. My fingers clutch at it, the metal feeling cool in the front and warm where it had rested against my skin.

I sigh, not wanting to walk all the way back to the shop.

"I'll just take it back tomorrow," I mumble to myself.

I try to tuck it under the collar of my shirt, but as I move it, the clasp slips—I must not have closed it all the way. The necklace topples down the front of my chest, bouncing off my body. I scramble to catch it as a wave washes up, but I miss it in the air.

It drops into the wave, tumbling back with it toward the open sea.

"No," I shout, racing toward it.

I try three times to snatch it out of the water before I finally get my fingers around it. A wave crashes against me, knocking my feet out from under me, forcing me to drop my shoes as I fall into the water.

The ocean pulls me away from the shore, crashing me into the sand. I tumble over and over, slamming into the gritty sand under the water. My mouth fills with water and sand, and I try to catch a breath of air as I flip around.

Panic sets in when I realize I won't be able to reach the surface—I don't even know which way is up.

The hands around me do though.

Propelling us through the water, my savior races us toward the surface. I let him guide me, not even bothering to help kick. His movements are swift and purposeful—I cling to his arms as he rescues me.

When I open my eyes, I can breathe again, but the world around me isn't the gold tones of sunset along the sandy beach—it's blue.

"You're fine," he says to me. "Just stay calm, and I'll explain."

I suck in another breath, miraculously not drowning. My eyes grow wide as I watch the man who rescued me float in the water, breathing normally as if he weren't surrounded by ocean.

My eyes trail down his beaded hair, covered in shells, to his chest. A belt sits on his waist, covered in bits of fish scales.

"I'm Quay," he informs me. My eyes dart back up to his face. "I'm sure this must be strange to you, but you're safe here. I'll help you."

His hands circle around my wrists as I tread water. He moves slightly, mimicking my motions to stay put in the ocean. Except...he's not moving like I am. The man is moving his hips back and forth with one motion instead of two as if walking on a treadmill.

I glance down again, reevaluating my situation—those weren't fish scales on a belt—it was a tail.

Quay has a tail.

I clench my teeth together as I force my eyes to keep dropping until I can see my own tail.

My white and gray print dress with the beautiful, luxurious sleeves is gone. My belt has washed away in the current and been replaced with a tail.

"Look at me," Quay squeezes my wrists as I begin to panic. "Tell me your name."

"Cara."

"Cara, look at me," he replies. When I don't, his hand darts up, catching my chin until I meet his ice-blue eyes. "You were pulled into the sea. You've been given a gift."

"A tail?" I ask in horror.

"You would have died in the water today had the sea not taken pity on you," he informs me. "You were transformed into a mermaid so that you would survive—you've been found worthy, Cara."

He drops his hand, leaving my face feeling exposed.

"Come, I have much to show you." He turns to swim away, still holding my wrist in one hand. "I'm bringing you to my mother—she's the queen of this part of the sea—she'll be able to explain this to you better."

"I need to get my legs back. I have to go home."

"Yes, the queen will help you." I find it curious that he refers to his mother by her title, but I don't say anything.

He smiles softly, nodding to get me moving. His eyes are narrow, but long—almost cat-like.

I follow along quietly, figuring out how to use my tail as he moves us along. I don't know which way land is, but

I imagine we're swimming further and further away from it.

I'm grateful I left my laptop at home today—it would be destroyed at this point. As it is, I'll need a new cell phone now. At least I didn't have any money on me—just the debit card I got a few months ago when I opened my bank account to start saving for a car to take to college next fall.

Fish swim all around us as we dive deeper in the water. I start to realize just how similar we look when a lionfish darts by me.

"You make a lovely mermaid, by the way," Quay looks back, admiring my new body. I blink, unsure of what to say.

His tail is similar to mine, covered in stripes and leafy parts. He almost looks like he found several giant blue beta fish and sewed their tails onto his. A few spikes stick up off the back of his tail, and I reach behind me to examine my own tail—I look like a human-sized lionfish.

I'm incredibly grateful for the sports bra I wore today, though it stands out in stark contrast to the more muted colors of my tail—no way of hiding this, I suppose.

He notices me frowning.

"Would you like some seaweed?" he asks.

"What?" I ask as he stops to face me. He refuses to take his eyes off mine.

"I noticed you looking at your attire. Perhaps it is not

to your liking? I offered you seaweed as a way to change your *iluse*."

"*Iluse?*" I ask, wondering if I'd have an easier time talking to a dolphin.

He motions to my chest without looking down.

"Oh," I catch on. "Oh! Yes, I would like seaweed."

Anything to cover up would be helpful.

Quay guides us further down in the water toward a seaweed garden. He lets me float while he gathers an armful of the water plants for me. The merman drapes them over his forearm, letting each piece have its own resting place. He hovers by my side, holding it out to me, facing the same direction I am to give me space.

I mumble something as I take them and quickly tuck the pieces in and around my sports bra to conceal it while he stares into the distance at my side—wearing light colors to match my dress turned out to not be so helpful today. I wrap pieces around me as low as I can go and still have it tucked into the wire around my bra as I bat my curly hair back.

I didn't realize it was possible to have a bad hair day while floating under the ocean—so much for mermaid hair being perfect.

"So this is an *iluse*, huh?" I ask when I'm done.

"Yes, mermaid," he addresses me. "Are you ready to go?"

This time, he lets me swim on my own, following along beside him.

"Quay, I can't be a mermaid," I blurt out.

"What do you mean? You're doing splendidly."

"I have to return to the surface," I say, squishing my childhood dreams.

"You have business beneath the sea, Cara," he looks back at me. "You're here for a reason. Shouldn't you explore what that is?"

He looks at me curiously.

"It's not right to waste a gift," he informs me.

"Destroying my cell phone is a gift all of a sudden?"

He furrows his brow when I mention my phone.

"A what?" he questions, nose wrinkled.

"Cell phone," I inform him. "It's a device you call people on—a way to communicate."

"Like a conch?"

"Umm, not exactly." *What?*

"Then what is this device?"

I explain how a cell phone works to the dark merman. I consider fishing it out of my bag to show him, but with my luck, I'd drop it to the bottom of the sea and never be able to find it again…not that it will work, even if I *do* get out of the ocean.

"So exactly like a conch," he replies. "You whisper a name into it, and then the message, and the shell locks out everyone else until it's delivered to the right person. Then your words fizzle away like seafoam."

I'd have to remember that next time I'm collecting shells on my walk home from work.

"Cara, look!" Quay shouts, swimming up in the water.

He bends his fingers so that his body waves as he moves. I push hard on my tail, trying to keep up. I tip my fingers up and down like I did as a child when my dad drove me home from school on his day off, and I stuck my fingers out of the window. I bounce mercilessly in the water until I hold my fingers straight.

"Look here," he says pointing to a tiny sea turtle.

He moves his hand near it, dropping a chain down so that it looks like the small creature was wearing it. Quay lifts it away as stealthily as a magician.

"Is that my necklace?" I gasp. "I was trying to catch it when I fell in."

"It's not yours, Cara," he grins. "Yours is around your neck. I slipped it on when I caught you."

He swims closer to me as my hand flies to my throat.

"This one is mine. It's an octopus, see?" Quay cocks an eyebrow at me. "It's a similar shape though, so I see how you could mistake it."

I'm impressed that he managed to get it around my neck without me noticing. Of course, I was rolling around in a rip tide, so that might have something to do with it.

"I also thought you might like to see the baby turtle."

"It was adorable," I reply, eyes roaming behind him to see where the creature swam off to, but I have no luck finding it.

"Come, there are more of them near the palace. Is there anything else you would like to see along the way?"

I'm not here for a sightseeing adventure. I'm here to meet the queen and see if she can help me get my legs back.

Then again, the pod of dolphins swimming toward us could make for a cool experience.

"What about them?" I ask, pointing toward the dolphins.

Silently, he swims ahead. I follow as closely as I dare. For a second, I consider catching a ride on his tail but then I realize he's a merman, not a dolphin.

The pod surrounds us, chattering. Quay nods to me as he holds out a hand, allowing a dolphin to slip under his waiting fingers. The moment a gray dorsal fin passes by, he takes off, darting through the water.

CHAPTER *Two*

A DOLPHIN SWIMS MY WAY. WHEN I WAS YOUNGER, I HAD the chance to swim with them on vacation once, so I reach out, prepared to catch a ride. The dolphin playfully races through the water, following Quay and it's friend.

Take me to the surface, I will it.

As if reading my mind, we dart up. I squint my eyes closed as we hit the top of the ocean, breaking into the fresh air. The dolphin carries me a few feet before going under the waves.

"Again," I say, encouraging it to surface one more time.

Obliging, we bounce back to the world I know and I look around as quickly as I can.

Land.

I can't reach it though. Not like this. Even if I did, I'd still have fins, so the sea queen is my best bet.

We dive back under the water, swimming low to the ground. If I had feet, I could have skidded to a stop like a parachuter running along the ground after jumping out of a plane.

Quay looks winded when I finally let go of the dolphin, allowing it to join its pod again.

"Are you okay?" I ask, concerned that my guide might pass out on the ocean floor.

"Fine, Cara. How was your swim with Maladai?" He rests a hand on his chest, offering me a weak grin.

"How far did you say the palace is?" I ask skeptically.

"Not too far," he replies. "Shall we continue?"

I nod, letting him guide me again. We swim slower to accommodate him for a few minutes.

"Do you swim with dolphins often?"

"Only when I have to get somewhere quickly. They're much faster than mer are."

We swim for a while in silence. The seaweed ripples under us. Stretching my hand out, I let it dance on my skin, tickling my palm.

"Ah, we have a visitor," Quay murmurs as a group of small mer children swim toward us.

"Prince Quay!" they shout as we draw near. They look shocked and thrilled to see the prince.

Several of them collide with him, slamming into his chest and wrapping themselves around his tail. His laughter is deep and melodic.

"What are you doing here?" an older girl I assume is their sister or babysitter asks. She looks at me critically.

Tipping her head toward him, she mumbles. "Should you be out here?"

I smile at the children as they stare at me curiously.

"This is my new friend, Cara. She's from the surface and I'm bringing her to my mother to help her get her legs back," he stresses the words, carefully pronouncing everything.

"She's a human?" the girl's face lights up. She turns to me, smiling. She nods. "Well, we're very pleased to see you."

"Thank you?" I pose my response as a question. *I think.*

She looks like she wants to swim over and shake my hand. Instead, she puts her hand on Quay's strong upper arm.

"Prince Quay will take very good care of you, I'm sure." She turns back to the group of mer children. "Come along, we need to let the prince do his job now."

"But Maianda!" they protest as she quickly turns them around and pushes them forward.

"Not another word," she says bitingly. "We're not disturbing the prince on his birthday."

"It's your birthday?" I ask, turning to him. He looks less strained now as he begins to swim again.

He smiles softly, glancing down.

"It is."

"How old are you?" I ask, expecting some number that's incredibly high.

"Eighteen," he replies as we swim. The children jabber about him in the background, but I don't catch their words, other than *needs to find a human.*

"That's it?" I instantly reply, shocked. I nearly reach up to cover my mouth when I realize I just blurted that out. He chuckles at me.

"What were you expecting me to say, Cara?"

"I don't know," I try not to blush. "All the stories I've heard say that mermaids and mermen live to be hundreds of years old. I assumed this was one of those teen vampire situations where you looked my age but were really four hundred twenty."

He turns back to me, shock written across his face.

"I was clearly born into the wrong collection," he smirks at me. "I should have been a vampire...whatever that is."

I would tease him about missing a pop culture phenomenon, but it's never impressed *me* either.

"How long *do* you live then?" I question, trying to avoid explaining what a vampire is supposed to be—I have a feeling the best explanation I can come up with involves a shark's teeth.

A long pause follows and I wonder if he's recently lost someone. When he finally answers, it sounds like a struggle.

"Most live into their eighties," he replies.

"I'm sorry," I whisper, swimming closer to him. I put my hand on his shoulder. "I didn't mean to bring that up. I lost my grandpa not too long ago, so I know how much it hurts to lose someone."

He takes a deep breath and pats my hand.

"No, Cara, it's fine," he replies. "We're only a few minutes away from the palace now."

I remove my hand from his shoulder, following him as he guides me to his home. It strikes me as funny that I'm so trusting of this merman that I just met. On the surface, I'd never go anywhere with a guy I didn't know.

"There's a starfish down there," Quay changes the conversation. "They say if you wish on it, it will come true."

"Well, in that case, I wish to go home," I pretend to wish on it. "Not that I'm not having a lovely time, I just really need to make it home before my parents get worried."

I'm sure I've already missed dinner. My family is probably out looking for me right now—too bad I can't text them that I'm running late.

"What did you wish for?" I ask.

"I have a birthday wish today that I'm using on everything," he replies. "It's the same thing I wish for every year on my birthday—I'd like another year."

"Always a good request," I giggle. "So what do mermen do to celebrate their birthday under the sea?"

"We usually dress up in our shoulder armor and *sarasas* and spend time with the mer we care about."

"And yet you were randomly near the surface just in time to save me?" I question. I add slyly, "Quay, were you meeting a mermaid up there? Am I keeping you from some secret rendezvous?"

"No, nothing like that." He looks back at me. "I think I was in precisely the right place at the right time. I couldn't have asked for anyone more beautiful to spend my birthday with."

Is he flirting with me?

"I suppose you don't have cake down here," I mumble ridiculously. "And certainly no candles. Do you sing?"

"Sing?" He stops swimming and turns to face me. "Your customs are very strange, Cara. Usually, the entire kingdom celebrates the prince's birthday, but never on the eighteenth—it's a day meant for transition for the royal line."

"Oh? Do you take over for your parents or something? Am I suddenly swimming in a king's presence?"

"I have a test to pass today. We're here," Quay informs me as we swim up over a ridge.

The palace looks like it's been built out of the treasure from a thousand sunken ships. It shines in the light pouring down through the surface of the ocean, reflecting back at me like a watch on the wrist of a man on the bus reading his newspaper without realizing he's blinding everyone each time he turns the page.

"This is where I live," Quay tells me, guiding me through the front door.

Everything inside sparkles as well. Jellyfish sit at the top of the room, glowing. Seahorses hold onto the pieces of seaweed in the corner. A school of fish quietly glides around the entryway.

"Ah, this is my stingray, Matumb." He reaches out his hand, cuddling the stingray. "You may pet him if you like."

I've fed stingrays before at the aquarium. I reach out, touching its velvety skin. He flaps his wings at me playfully. Quay pulls a dead fish out of the pouch attached to his belt and feeds his pet. Patting it on the head, he sends it off.

"Your Highness," a merman soldier appears in front of us. He gives the prince a sharp nod—I assume it's their version of a bow. "Is there anything I can do for you?"

He almost sounds sad as he asks.

"No, my friend. All is well. Would you inform the queen that I have returned and have brought a friend with me that needs to speak to her."

The soldier's eyes light up similarly to the way the mermaid's had out in the open waters. He nods again, swimming back out of the room.

"Come, you should see the palace while you still can," Quay offers me his hand.

The first room we swim into looks to be some kind of parlor. There are holes in the ceiling that allow the light to shine through. I imagine they're magnificent in the moonlight as well.

"What is that?" I ask, pointing to a bumpy chair.

"That's a lounging couch. We sit on it," he explains as if humans stand all the time. "You may try it if you like."

I bite back my remarks and swim over to it, settling myself between two of the bumps.

"No," he laughs. "Well, *yes*, we *do* sit on it like that when there are more than one of us, but *this* is the proper way."

Quay reaches around my back, scooping up my tail. I suck in a breath as he turns my body, spreading me out over the couch so that my head rests on one bump and my tail hangs over the other. It's surprisingly comfortable.

His hands linger on me, resting on my shoulder and what I suppose would be my knees if I still had them.

"More comfortable?" he asks, grinning over me.

"It is. Is this how you sleep down here?"

"We have beds, just like in your stories."

So he does *know that we don't stand all the time.*

A strand of his shell-clad hair falls in front of him, but he doesn't bother to brush it back as he stares.

"You've read our stories?"

"Sleeping girls and princes, girls who forget their feet…I've seen a few from the old books that fell off sailor's ships generations ago."

"You've read Cinderella?" I laugh.

"Do you know any mer tales?" he shakes his head playfully.

Quay taps my tail, prompting me to set it down on the far side of the couch. He swims around it and sits next to me where my tail had been. Leaning in, he rests his elbows and arms on the bump between us. With his chest pressed against his arms, he puts his chin down on his forearms.

I lean back, scooting down in the seat to see him better.

"A few," I say coyly. If he wants to play games, I can play games. We might be on *his* playing field, but I won't let him have home court advantage.

"My mother likes to tell mermaid stories," I say casually. "She still tells them to my baby cousin every time we babysit. My brother and I may be too old, but I always enjoy listening whenever my cousin comes over for the night."

"You have a brother?"

"I do. Are you the only prince, or are there more?" I challenge.

"I had bothers once," he replies, looking away.

Maybe that was why he was sad earlier.

"I'm sorry," I offer. "Brothers are a wonderful thing to have. I wouldn't trade mine for the world."

"It was hard to let them go. I would have traded places with them if I could have."

"How did you lose them?" I hope I'm not overstepping.

"It's a long story. I'll explain later. For now, you should come with me. We need to get you ready to meet the queen—everything is pageantry down here, and your appearance is no exception."

He holds a hand to me, carefully taking mine in his. We swim down the hall to a room filled with accessories.

"This is our guest closet," Quay says, tucking his braids back over his shoulders. "Whenever we have people who don't live in the palace here and an event comes up, they may borrow pieces."

He swims me to a table covered in headpieces. Shells are scattered everywhere. Bits of coral and driftwood mix with shells and pearls, surrounded by netting and crystals.

"Your *iluse* looks fine, but if you'd like one of ours, you're welcome to it." He motions to a rack near the wall. I nearly select one, but then I realize I might not have anywhere to change and I'm definitely not switching bras in front of him.

"This is fine," I mumble demurely. "What are these?"

He squints his eyes playfully at me as I change the subject.

"You may adorn your hair any way you'd like. Pick one out and I'll help you put it on."

My fingers dance over the crystals and shells. I finally pick one out that's got blue crystals mixed with blue and green shells. Quay takes the one I point to and swims behind me. His tail occasionally pulses against mine when he flicks it to stay floating in the same spot.

The shells aren't as heavy as I expect, though that could be because the water makes everything lighter. Once he has it situated, he swims in front of me, examining the placement on my head. He turns, twisting at the waist to pick up several strands of pearls. His abdomen ripples tightly with the movement, muscles moving gracefully.

"A mermaid should always wear pearls," he explains. "They show off her hair."

Quay swims behind me again, working his fingers through my hair expertly. I nearly shudder at his touch. I've always loved when people play with my hair, but it's somehow more luxurious underwater.

"You're very good at this," I comment, tipping my head back slightly into his touch.

"All mermen know how to design hair. It is a sign of love and respect to the mermaids in our lives."

That is the most divine thing I've ever heard.

"That's so interesting. On the surface, guys wouldn't be caught dead knowing what a braid is, much less anything else."

"Your men sound like fools," Quay mutters.

I can't say I disagree.

"It's a shame you can't come to the surface and open a shop—you'd clean up!"

"Clean up?" I'm sure he's wrinkling his nose behind me but I can't see him.

"That just means that you'd be very popular and make a lot of money," I explain. "If you opened a shop and did people's hair, you'd do really well for yourself."

"I'd be a king?" he jokes. "Perhaps I should try it."

He weaves the pearls around the crown, dropping them in my hair so they settle above my eyebrows and ears, stretching around to the back. I close my eyes as he works.

"I'm very sorry this happened to you, Cara. You don't deserve this."

"I'll survive," I reply with a smile. I open my eyes. "You and your mother will help me get back and I'll calm my family down. I'm sure they're panicking right now. I honestly hope they didn't find the shoes I dropped though—that would scare them too much."

"Why is that?"

"I dropped them next to the water. I don't want them thinking I drowned or something."

"I see. All done," Quay says, swimming in front of me to examine his work again. His jaw drops when he sees me. "You look like a mer princess, Cara."

My eyebrows shoot up. There's no way.

He sees my disbelief and purses his lips. Swirling his hand in the water, he creates a large bubble. My image reflects back at me—he's right—I look incredible.

Turning, I examine myself like I do when I'm trying on clothes at the mall. The spikes on my tail accent the brown, orange, and red colors of my scales. Everything makes my dark skin pop. My hair retained its curliness and the pearls look incredible as they sit in my flowing locks. I tip my head—same nose, same pouty lips, but my eyes look larger than usual and more pronounced as if my makeup has changed slightly.

I reach out for my reflection, accidentally popping the bubble. It bursts, taking my image with it.

"You look striking," he repeats. "I don't know how the kingdom will let you go—you are a treasure."

He swims closer. His eyes are mesmerizing in that icy blue tone. He gets so close that I could dart forward and kiss him, *which would be awesome* because the *last thing* I need to do right now is fall for a *merman* and then go back to land.

Pull it together, Cara.

"Do all of the mermaids dress like this?" I ask, turning back to the rows of hairpieces on the table behind Quay.

"Most, yes." He swims beside me, running his fingers over the pieces on the table. "You may keep those for as long as you like. They are a gift."

"Oh, no, I couldn't. I'll return them when I go home," I insist. I'd probably never get the shells and pearls untangled from my hair without his help anyway once I hit the open air.

"Really," he counters. "I want you to have them."

"That's very kind of you, Quay."

"Your Highness, your mother is ready to see you," a merman hovers in the doorway.

"Thank you, we'll be right there," Quay says without turning to face the merman. "I must explain things to you, Cara."

I nod, waiting for his instructions. Surely the queen must be as kind as her son, but I hold my breath, waiting for the shoe to drop.

"I will introduce you when we go in. My mother and the others will likely ask you a series of questions—just answer as best as you can. Do not ask anything yourself unless she gives you permission. She will know why you are here and will explain what you need to do."

"All right," I say softly. "She's nice, isn't she?"

"Everyone loves and respects her. She is the most beloved queen the kingdom has seen in a long time," Quay replies. "Come."

CHAPTER *Three*

I FOLLOW QUAY THROUGH THE HALLWAYS, STAYING CLOSE by his side. His fingers brush against mine a few times, but he doesn't flinch, so I hold myself still.

Do not kiss a merman, do not kiss a merman, do not kiss a merman.

The throne room is dazzling. We swim in and the room comes to life. A number of mermaids and mermen hover on the right side of the room, watching us enter.

The mer queen sits on a throne that has clearly been brought in from an old sunken ship and must have belonged to the richest sea captain in the world. They've adorned it with shells and crystals. Sea plants grow beneath it in a colorful rainbow.

"Hello, child," the queen says. Her voice is high and airy.

I'm shocked at how young she looks to have a son turning eighteen. Her hair is long and luxurious, but she has the same cat-eyes Quay has.

I bow my head sharply like I saw the soldiers do earlier, hoping I got their sign of respect correct. When I look up, she's smiling with approval.

"What is your name?"

"Cara, your majesty." It's strange calling someone that if it's not the tabby cat that lives by the pier where I work.

"Cara, where do you come from?"

"Land." I'd give her the name of my coastal town, but that would just lead to a long—and likely confusing—conversation.

"How did you come to be here?" she asks skeptically.

"I dropped a necklace into the ocean by accident. When I was trying to catch it, the waves pulled my feet out and I ended up in the water."

"You have a tail," the queen points out the obvious.

"The woman who gave me the necklace said it had the power to turn me into a mermaid. I didn't believe her, but apparently it was true."

The queen nods to her court with a smile before turning back to me.

"Do you know why you are here, Cara of land?" she asks. Her hair floats in front of her, but it only adds to the majesty of her presence.

Strands of pearls cover her hair—much like mine—but they also stretch from her shoulder armor to the cuffs around her wrists, creating a cape effect. Her crown is made of gold and stretches high above her, sparking as the last of daylight filters through the water. The room seems alive with color, even though it's fading.

"Your son said you could help me return home. I need to get my legs back and return to my family before they become too worried about me."

"I see," she hums.

If she weren't so lovely and gentle looking, the soft way she is speaking might freak me out. She's like some distant queen in a movie that is removed from her subjects in the storyline but can destroy them all with a single word—I'm shocked she isn't glowing.

"You are here for a purpose, Cara of land," the queen addresses me. "I need you to help me complete a task for my son. Help him and I'll see to it that you make it back to land when it's all over so your parents can find you."

"Anything, your majesty. I just want to go home."

"Very good," the queen nods. She calls her son. "Quay."

He swims closer to me, his energy electric. He seems almost nervous.

"Yes?" she asks her son vaguely.

"Yes, mother," he nearly cringes next to me. His tail flicks impatiently in the water as his fingers close in on his palms.

"We must begin the ceremony immediately," the queen addresses the room, smiling.

"Ceremony?" I ask. Quay looks at me, scared—I spoke when I wasn't supposed to.

"Yes, dear, it's my son's birthday. We must perform a ceremony—"

"I'm not marrying him or something, am I?" I blurt out, suddenly worried about what I might have walked —*swam*—into by mistake.

"Of course not. A mer prince cannot marry a human girl," the queen remarks haughtily. "All you have to do is stay there and Quay will do the rest. We're here as witnesses."

She spreads her arms out in front of her, motioning to the sea floor we're hovering over. Quay slowly backs out of my line of sight, but the queen demands my attention.

"Go prepare yourself for your test, son. Cara," she addresses me, "you look lovely. I see my son has taken you to our guest closet. Do you like your headpiece?"

"Yes, your majesty."

"It's very fitting for the ceremony," she says. "All of my sons have been through this on their eighteenth birthdays, though I think today will be different with your presence."

"I can come back if you'd like to keep it—"

"No child, we wouldn't have it any other way," the queen quickly cuts me off. "My son must perform a special ceremony, you see. All mer princes must complete the ceremony on their eighteenth year of birth."

She motions me forward.

"Come, join me."

I swim forward, unsure of what to do. She reaches out her hand to me, long fingers beckoning me closer. Placing my hand in her's, she pulls me toward her throne.

"Now, jellyfish, Quay will need help with this. It's tradition to ask someone from the room to join him—he will choose you—you're the most lovely one here." I blush at her remarks. "He and I will guide you. Just follow along—this will go a long way toward getting you back to your parents too."

I turn as Quay enters the room again, this time, singing. His shoulder armor is now covered in blue shells, similar to mine. Pearls stretch across his chest from one shoulder to another.

"It's time to begin the Sinking," the queen announces as happily as if she'd just been handed a winning lottery ticket.

It's a strange name for a ceremony, but whatever.

Quay dances in the water, spinning in a way so that his hair flies out from him. It dips gracefully in the water. The sword on his belt loops out majestically as he moves. Some of the mermaids in the audience sway along with him, humming with his words. The shells move with him, dancing over his body.

"Each of my sons has taken a turn trying to complete the ceremony, starfish," the queen whispers in my ear. "They've all failed. Tonight, Quay will try to complete the ceremony—he's come farther than any of my other sons have come, and I have great hopes for him."

She pushes my back, sending me into the open waters of the throne room toward Quay. He notices and swims over to me, never breaking his song.

Quay holds a hand to me and I tentatively take it. He guides me to the center of the room, singing an enchanting song. His voice is so lovely that I begin to wonder if he's a siren in disguise.

I sway with him as he guides me through the water. It's almost like prom night again as the last rays of light dance through the hole in the roof, sparkling against bits of debris in the water.

Definitely like prom.

Quay slows us, pulling me closer to him. He places my hands on his collarbone and draws me to him. His singing stops but the other mer pick up the tune, enchanting the waters with their voices.

"Cara," he murmurs, looking deep into my eyes.

The queen said it wasn't a marriage ceremony, but this is getting awfully romantic. I swallow hard, wondering how to put some space between us.

"Three of my sons have tried to complete the Sinking," the queen announced, breaking the trance. She swims toward us. "Three have failed and paid with their lives. Tonight, Quay will not fail.

"My son has brought a human to this palace as the curse foretold he must," she continues.

My skin prickles under the water—I was *brought* here.

Quay's grip around me tightens as his face goes slack.

No. Bad.

"My sons have been cursed since their childhood," the queen continues. "They've been doomed to die on the eve of their eighteenth year—"

"I'm sorry, Cara," Quay whispers.

I struggle to free myself.

"—if they did not complete the Sinking," the queen swims toward us as I pull back. Quay clamps down on my wrists and I worry they might shatter.

"Settle, anemone," the sea queen lectures me.

Anemone.

My mind flashes back to a few hours ago when the old woman pawned that necklace off on me—only it wasn't an old woman—it was the sea queen in disguise. She *planned this.*

"Why am I here?" I yell, struggling to get away from Quay. I pull one hand free, desperately trying to claw him off of my other wrist. Tears spring to my eyes but all they do is leak out into the water surrounding me.

"Quay, let me go!" I beg, sobbing.

"The last son of the reigning queen must break the curse by midnight or he too shall perish."

"Break the curse," the audience cheers, lending their support to the prince.

He pulls on me.

"Quay, please," I duck my head as I beg, hoping he'll see my fear and spare me.

If it's his life or mine, there's no way I'll win.

"Quay, please, you promised you'd help me. You saved me before."

"He saved you, child, because I instructed him to," the queen silences me, grabbing my chin and forcing me to look at her. "The curse says the princes must Sink a human in the heart of the sea before midnight on the day of his birth.

"Until this point, no human has survived the trip to the heart of the sea—the palace—and I've lost three other sons to this curse. I will not lose Quay, not even for *your* sake. I'm sorry you have to give your life for this, but I'll see to it that your family finds your body when we're done, legs back in place."

"You horrible witch!" I scream, still pulling against Quay, hoping to save my life. Though, even *if* I free myself, one of the other mer will stop me.

These mermaids and mermen will see to it that I drown in the heart of their kingdom to save their prince's life.

"I've done bad things in my life," the queen admits, "but always to help my collection or my sons. I'm sorry I had to trick you and bring you into the sea, but it's the only way to save my son's life, and I regret nothing if it means he lives past tonight."

I understand the need to protect loved ones, but she's murdering me to do it. She threw me into the sea and transformed me into a mermaid just to bring me to my death.

"Cara, stop struggling," Quay commands gently.

"I have a family," I shriek. "I have parents and a brother and a little cousin who depend on me. I'm going to college next year and I'm saving for a car to get there. I get straight A grades in all of my classes and I volunteer at the animal shelter twice a month. Please!"

"I can tell you are a good person, child, but it makes no difference," the queen responds lifelessly. "Quay must kill a human in the heart of the sea and he must do it now to survive. Thank you for your sacrifice."

"No!" I pull, ripping my hand away from Quay.

"Take her necklace," the queen instructs as I struggle.

"I cannot," Quay says, hands up as if he were surrendering. "I cannot kill the girl, Mother, I'm sorry."

"You *can* and you *will*, Quay. You will not leave us tonight. I've gone through far too much and given up everything for you to survive—you can't let her go!"

"I can't kill her, Mother," Quay looks devastated as I look over my shoulder, swimming to the door. A merman stops me. I try to dart around him, but can't.

"I have paid with my life for this, Quay. Both of our lives will be in vain if you don't do this now," she screeches. The other mer look horrified at her revelation.

"I care about her," he says quietly. I want to gag.

"You can't be in love with her, you idiot, you've known her for three hours."

"I didn't say *love*, Mother, but I'm drawn to her."

"She's a human," his mother protests. "And you both will be dead by morning—she'll never make it out of the sea. You must do this and live. I'll find you another to be drawn to."

Quay swims quietly toward me. I bite back a sob, grinding my teeth so hard that I can't hear anymore as my body shakes with the effort. I writhe violently as the merman holds my wrists.

"Hold still," I read Quay's lips. He comes at me with a knife in hand. Even if I can reach his sword, I doubt I'll make it in time.

Quay takes my hands from the merman blocking the door and roughly pulls me away. He turns back to his mother, knife still raised at me.

This is it. My life is over.

I spent my childhood dreaming of being a mermaid and now I will die as one. My family will find my body washed up along the beach somewhere and I will be gone forever.

Quay turns back to me, obviously having said something to his mer friends.

"Go," he commands, pushing me at the door.

I stare.

"Go!" he shouts, turning back to fight off any mer that challenge him. His shoulders hunch in pain, but I don't care one bit about what ails him.

I don't question his willingness to die at the hands of whatever curse he suffers from. I swim. I dart around the palace, desperate to find the door. When I do, I push my way to freedom in the almost-dark of night.

CHAPTER *Four*

I HAVE NO IDEA WHERE I'M GOING OR WHERE TO SWIM.

The queen said I wouldn't survive the night and she also said she'd paid for this with her life, so I assume that means whatever she did to curse me into this form probably won't last longer than a few hours.

I need to make sure I can get to the surface, but I'm also aware that the higher I am, the easier I am to spot in the distance.

I swim. I don't know where, I don't know how far, but I swim as hard as I can.

When I feel faint, I bury myself in a kelp forest and pray none of the mer think to look there. I hear them in the distance as they search for the human girl who will trade her life for the life of their prince.

He can drown for all I care.

Things glow in the dark—fish and jellyfish that capture their prey by drawing them in with their light.

That's what Quay did to me—drew me in with his light.

Too bad the merman had fangs after all—rows and rows of vicious teeth under the chiseled façade.

Stop thinking about him, I command myself.

"Stay quiet," Quay's voice fills my head—a trick my mind is playing on me.

"Go away," I mutter at the vision. "Traitor."

"I tried to save you, I'm not a traitor," Quay says, appearing next to me. I scream as he clamps his hand over my mouth.

"Quiet, Cara," he demands. "I'm here to help you. I'll take you back."

"You mean you'll kill me," I wrench away from him. "This is just another part of your plan, isn't it, you eel?"

"I look like an eel to you?" he frowns.

"You look like a murderer," I reply, trying to find an escape.

"Cara, I wouldn't have let you go if I didn't intend on saving you. It isn't fair that you should die for me. I'll go to be with my brothers—it's a fate I've already reconciled with for myself. I had hope of survival for a few hours but I could never hurt you like that."

He looks sincere, but I don't believe a word he says.

"Let me take you back to your home," he requests. "We have to hurry before your tail wears off and you can no longer breathe underwater."

I *knew* it.

"I'll protect you from my mother and the others.

They'll be all right without me—they already said good-bye. I'll take you to shore and then I'll return and make my peace with my fate on my own."

He's good. He's really good.

"Why don't you make your peace *over there*," I point. "I don't want your help."

"You need my help to return to land, Cara. You don't know where to go."

Moonlight sparkles down through the water, casting an eerie look over the merman. I nearly want to reach out and brush his long hair back from his face, but then I remember that he is the enemy.

"I will not willingly give my life up to you," I tell him.

"I'm not asking you to, Cara," he replies. "I just want you to let me fix what my mother has done to protect me. It is my duty to make it right. Let me do this one thing before the curse takes me."

I have no choice. I don't know how to get home, the glowing creatures are out to get me, and I'll die with or without Quay by my side, so I might as well drown while staring at his abs.

"Fine," I grumble.

He darts away from me, whispering for me to follow. I take off after him, racing through the dark.

I stay close to his tail so that I don't lose him in the darkness. I glide into his slipstream, making it easier to keep up.

"What was supposed to happen to me, Quay?" I ask bitterly.

"I was supposed to take your necklace," he says quietly. He looks like he wants to stop to talk to me, but we can't risk pausing and being found. "When removed, it takes away your ability to breath underwater—you turn back into a human.

"At that point, I was supposed to drown you," he concludes.

"I suppose you were going to add your own dramatic flair?" I question.

"My back up plan was to kiss you and try to give you enough air to get you to the surface," he admits, "if that is what you mean by flair."

I most certainly do *not* want to kiss him—but his lips are so enchanting.

"Hurry, Cara, we need to get you to the shore."

"How often do you go to the shore?" I ask, trying to learn anything I can use against him later.

"Never. It is forbidden."

"But you found me today," I protest.

"My mother sent me to fetch you. The only time we go to the shore is to get the human we need for the ceremony. Her plan succeeded this time—or would have if I could have followed it," he says dismally. "I just knew I couldn't live with myself with your blood on my hands."

"You said you felt drawn to me," I comment. "What

does that mean?"

"I don't know," he replies. "I feel we have a connection. That's all I can tell you."

A noise sounds in the distance—the mermen are coming for us.

"We need to hide," Quay says, looking around. "There. A cavern."

He grabs my hand, pulling me down in the water whether I like it or not. I allow him to swim us into the cave.

Inside, we find a darkness so overwhelming that it's a shock to the system when light begins to glow around us.

"Bioluminescence," he informs me. "When the algae is disturbed, that happens."

Everything glows around us as we hover in the water.

"They can't see it outside, can they?" I ask.

"No, we're too far inside the cave."

He enfolds me in his arms, holding me to his chest. I try not to cringe, though I keep my elbows firmly in place between him and me in case I need to push him away.

His hand settles on the small of my back around the spikes and frilly pieces of my tail—I honestly don't know how mermaids deal with this. It's one thing to have fins at the bottom, but extra offshoots everywhere?

It's pretty, but not worth it.

His fingers graze one of the fins making me gasp. I can't tell if it's horrifying or if it's incredible.

"I truly am sorry, Cara," he murmurs.

"So you've said."

He sighs.

"I'm willing to die to protect you, Cara. I hope you'll remember that one day when you think of me."

I'll be sure to thank him in my speech before the police check me into a facility for a seventy-two-hour hold after I tell them about all this.

"Stay here, I'll go check."

I grab his wrist, eyes wide.

"I'm not bringing them back here, Cara," he groans. "If I were going to kill you in front of them, I would have done it at the palace. If I needed to kill you in the cavern, I would have brought you directly here instead of to my mother. I am on your side."

He swims away, leaving me in the glow of the cave.

He makes a good point.

Still, I look for anything I can use as a weapon should I need it.

When he returns, he's alone.

"They're gone," he announces, holding out his hand. "We need to move faster or we won't make it in time."

Time for me to turn back into a human or time for him to die? Maybe both.

"When will I….*transform*?" I ask as we swim back into the ocean.

"Soon," he replies. "We don't have long."

"Will my transformation and your...um, death be at the same time?"

"I do not know, but I don't think so. I believe you'll transform first. I have until the end of the day, but I don't think your necklace will hold you much longer, which is why we need to swim faster. Please, Cara. I'm sure you're exhausted and you're still learning your tail, but please hurry."

He sounds terrified that we're not going fast enough. I push, flipping my tail as hard as I can. My control over direction leaves something to be desired, but with my hand in his, I manage to go in the right direction, despite bumping into him several times.

"Quay," I gasp, finding it hard to breathe. "I have to slow down."

I cough, trying to catch my breath.

"No," he whispers in shock, halting. He adds dismally,"It's time."

"What?" I squeak out between coughs.

"You're turning back into a human, Cara. Hold on, I have to get you to the surface."

He grabs me around the waist, practically throwing me over his shoulder as he darts toward the waves overhead. I start gagging, choking on the water as I transform.

Everything hurts as my scales tear away from me.

I scream in pain.

Chapter Five

"Hold on, Cara," he instructs as water goes up my nose, burning the entire inside of my head. "Almost there."

My nails dig into his back as I fight to survive.

Just as I think I'm going to black out, we hit the air.

My hair flops in front of my face and I fight to free myself from my new prison. Quay holds tightly to me with one arm and pokes at my face with his other hand, trying to help part my hair enough that air can enter my lips and heal my lungs.

I cough, spitting up water.

"You're safe," he murmurs, rubbing my back with the hand he was using to help with my hair. "You're on the surface now. You're safe."

I cling to him, letting him soothe me.

Miraculously, the merman saved me.

"Shh," he says softly. "We still have to get you home. Calm yourself down and try to breathe normally."

When I finally take my face out of his neck where I buried it, all I see is water. I look back at him in horror.

"We didn't quite make it, but I'll get you there," he promises.

He scoops my legs up in his arms and carries me toward the horizon, swimming on the surface.

"It's over there," he says. "It's just hard to see in the dark."

I see a space where the reflection on the water ends, and I assume that's land, but in the immense darkness, I can't be sure.

After a while, he struggles to stay above the water.

"Are you okay?"

"We don't swim up here much," he grunts in reply. "It's hard to stay above water."

"I can swim on my own—you can go back under."

"I'm not leaving you. We've come this far, and since this is the last thing I do, I want to do it right."

I notice part of my dress is still wrapped around me, covering my legs—I'm incredibly grateful whatever curse had wrapped me in scales had used my own garments to assist in the transformation.

"Then swim under the water next to me," I reply, wondering how many times I'm going to panic, thinking he's a shark about to bite me.

"No, we're fine," he pants. "We'll make it."

He dips lower in the water. I drop my hand into the ocean behind him and cup water onto his shoulders.

"Does this help?"

He smiles sadly at me.

"You're kind, Cara," he responds.

So, no, it's not helping. He doesn't stop me though, so I keep going, knowing it's meaningful to him that I'm trying to be helpful.

I pause between handfuls of water, not wanting to over do it. Every time the water touches his skin his lips tick up, or his eyes soften for a moment, closing slightly as he gives himself over to the water.

"I made the right choice," he says at one point during our journey. "You are the one that should live, Cara."

"So should live too, Quay."

There's no way I'm giving up my life for this though, so let's not even go there.

"You don't deserve this," I add. "You're a good merman."

"None of us deserved this, but it's our fate—our curse."

"There must be *something* that we can do," I protest. "There *has* to be a way to stop this."

"There is nothing that can stop this," he says sadly. "I wish though, that I had a chance to get to know you better, Cara of land."

"Funny, I was thinking the same thing about you, Quay, prince of the sea."

His smile nearly breaks my heart.

Quay looks behind me, smile morphing into relief.

"We're here," he says. "Just in time."

I turn to look, and he twitches under my movements.

The shore is there, right in front of me. I might even be able to reach the bottom if I put my feet down, though, with the waves, I don't dare let go of the merman carrying me to safety.

I slide my fingers across his shoulders, not wanting to say goodbye yet.

"Quay," I say, turning back to him.

He hunches over in the water, dipping me low into the waves. I gasp for air, reliving my transformation.

"Quay!" I shout as he starts to convulse.

"Go, Cara," he replies, pushing me away from him.

A wave catches me, hurdling me toward the shore as Quay shudders in the water.

"What's happening?" I demand, trying to get back to him.

"Go home, Cara," he tries to wave me off.

"Quay!"

"It's happening," he replies, heartbroken. "I don't want you to see me like this, please go."

"I'm not leaving you," I fight my way through the waves. "You took me home—now I'll take you home."

He starts thrashing in the water, bobbing up and

down in the waves. He's tossed like a buoy indicating the end of the swimming area in the ocean.

When I finally reach him, his entire body shakes.

I wonder if my transformation had looked this terrifying.

Wrapping an arm around him, I try to stabilize him in the water to make it the least painful I can. I can barely touch the bottom so I attempt to drag him into where I won't potentially drown.

"Quay, I'm here."

He reaches around me, attempting to ground himself with my body, using me as an anchor. His body twitches as his tail whips in the water around me.

Quay grunts, groaning in pain with every movement. He looks like he's snapping to the beat of a charged AED machine and someone is trying to revive him with panels on his chest. I nearly expect someone to scream *clear!*

His feet kick up from the water for a moment plunging back down into the black depths of the rough line of shells in the water. I hold tighter to him, just wanting to make his passing easier.

Wait.

Feet?

Sweet sunrise, the boy has legs!

"Quay!" I shout over the roar of the waves. "You have legs!"

His eyes pinch shut in pain.

"I know," he replies through gritted teeth.

"You're turning into a human?" I gape.

He attempts to nod, letting out a strangled yell of pain.

"Quay, you're human!" I repeat. "You're not dead, you're a human."

"They all turned…" he groans, "into humans and drowned."

"But you're not below the sea," I remind him, barely loosening my grip on his waist. "You're on land, Quay. You can't drown here."

"We're all cursed to die," he moans, convulsions slowing. "It will happen anyway, even above the sea."

"You're not going to die, Quay," I reply. "I've got you."

His breathing steadies as he practices long, deep breaths for the first time in his life. When he calms down, I brush his hair back as he leans back in my arms.

"I think you're safe, Quay. I think you survived."

"Go home, Cara. I'll be fine," he insists, still thinking he's going to keel over dead in front of me.

I duck down in the water with him.

"We're safe, your highness," I giggle. "We can reach out to your mother and let her know you're well. I mean, I don't particularly like her at this point since she's still trying to murder me, but maybe the fact that you didn't die in her palace will change her mind about me."

He finally focuses his piercing blue eyes on me.

His hands are wrapped around my shoulder and I reach up to move a lock of his shell-beaded hair back.

"You're safe. I'm safe. You saved me and now we're both free."

"*You* saved *me,* Cara. I honestly don't know how, but you did. " He puts his hand on his chest. "Thank you."

"We should get out of the water," I reply. Dark means feeding time for the small sharks that like to eat toward shore, and the last thing I need is to have something bite off Quay's new legs.

I move us toward the shore, helping him to get his feet under himself as we near a level where we'd either have to start walking or resort to crawling in on our knees.

The water slaps my backside before I can straighten and nearly sends me head first into the sand. I catch myself on Quay who hasn't found his land legs yet and nearly topples with me.

Thankfully his transformation has left him with something that looks a bit like a faded blue kilt wrapped around his waist. I help him up onto the shore where we both collapse.

Breathing is hard as we sit together, me curled up on his chest, tucked under his arm, and Quay sprawled out on his back. When we calm down, we're left under the stars with the ocean waves beating against the sand a few feet away.

"So," he breaks the silence. "This is land."

"This is land," I repeat, reaching up to rip the necklace off of my neck. "Looks like I'm about to have a lot to show you, Prince Quay."

He nods, taking it all in as his hand finds it's way to my hip, wrapped around my back as he cradles me against him.

I'm sure the world up here will be shocking to him.

The sand crunches in my hair—I'm going to need a hot shower when I get home to fix my salt-and-sand-crusted body. It's amazing how I can climb out of one body of water and desperately want to slip into another.

"I have a feeling I'm going to have a lot of explaining to do too," I reply. "Time to get our stories straight—I'm thinking that I dropped the necklace and got sucked out to sea and you were passing by on a canoe and fished me out of the drink."

Is it possible for him to *smell* like the sea?

"The drink?"

"The ocean," I correct myself. I'm really going to have to stop using half my vocabulary around the merman— around the *man*. "You can stay with my family until we figure out what to do about all of this. Maybe your mother can sell her soul again and get new magic to turn you back into a merman."

"Perhaps," he sounds skeptical. "I would like to see your world though, Cara."

"I'd like to show you." I pause for a moment, thinking through the day. "Hey, my wish on the starfish came true."

"Mine too," he chuckles for the first time since we climbed onto the sand. "Even my second and third wish came true."

"Oh? What was that?"

"My first wish was to survive the day. I have done that," he says. "My second wish was for my mother to not be able to silence you with the Sinking and here you are. And you already know my third wish."

"Do I?" I challenge.

"You had the same wish. To know each other better."

My eyes grow wide.

With my hand on his chest, rising in the air each time he takes a breath, and head curled into his strong shoulder that is surprisingly lacking in shoulder armor, I realize he's right—I'm glad I get to learn more about this mysterious merman.

A voice calls for me in the distance, searching for me well into the night.

"Uh oh," I add. "Time to go. Don't forget the story— you rescued me and we just made it back to shore."

He nods, allowing me to help pull him up—he's still not used to carrying his body weight and not being able to float everywhere.

"Ready to meet my family, your highness?"

Acknowledgments

Mermaid kisses to all of you fabulous readers! Thank you so much for joining me for Cara and Quay's story.

Cara has been such an interesting character for me and Quay is pretty different from most of the guys I've written, so it's been rather fun to explore with this story. I love being able to incorporate elements from the original Little Mermaid within this story in subtle ways in this novella which was originally created for the Of The Deep mermaid Anthology.

Thank you so much for all the love and artwork you've sent my way from The Sinking—it's breathtaking!

Special thanks to Yentl for being the first to fall for Cara and Quay…I know you have lots to say about these too, boo, and I appreciate it all!

Thank you to Elle and Jessica for all of your marvelous help as well!

Extra special thanks to Lauren for being an inspirational source in creating Cara's look for this story!

Mostly, thank you to my readers—without you, this story wouldn't exist and I'd be terribly sad to have never been able to meet Cara and Quay now that I've been able to get to know them.

I know you're all asking for more of Cara and Quay… stay tuned, more might be on the way! Until then, reach out on social media because I want to chat with you!

While you wait, be sure to check out my mermaid series, The Siren Wars Saga—you can read the first chapter right here inside the novella—*and* I'll tell you a little about my other series and books too!

Stay inspired!

-K.M. Robinson

WORLD PORTALS

Ready to learn exclusive facts about The Sinking and other K.M. Robinson Series?

World Portals are now available on
www.kmrobinsonbooks.com

Learn behind the scenes facts, watch videos, play games, check out our book filters, find out where to get bonus scenes, view fan art, and get access to other secrets we've hidden away inside the World Portals on the website.

The World Portals are constantly changing and information is being taken away and added all the time, so check back frequently for new content!

BONUS FACEBOOK FILTERS

Want to get your hands on some incredible Facebook filters for Siren Wars? Now you have the ability to get filters for the story, characters, etc right inside your phone.

You can use these on your photos, profile pictures, videos, and live broadcasts. All you have to do is like my author page and they will automatically show up in your filters!

I've even taken these clips and put them on Instagram Stories by saving them to my phone and uploading them to Instagram.

Visit www.facebook.com/kmrobinsonbooks to grab these filters for your photos, videos, and broadcasts! Bonus points for tagging me @kmrobinsonbooks so I can see how you're supporting The Siren Wars.

ABOUT THE AUTHOR

K.M. Robinson is a storyteller who creates new worlds both in her writing and in her fine arts conceptual photography. She is a marketing, branding and social media strategy educator who is recognized at first sight by her very long hair. She is a creative who focuses on photography, videography, couture dress making, and writing to express the stories she needs to tell. She almost always has a camera within reach. Visit her at her website: www.kmrobinsonbooks.com

CONNECT ON SOCIAL MEDIA

facebook.com/kmrobinsonbooks

instagram.com/kmrobinsonbooks

twitter.com/kmrobinsonbooks

Get free books and excerpts of other K.M. Robinson
books at excerpt.kmrobinsonbooks.com

ALSO BY K.M. ROBINSON

The Siren Wars Saga

Book One: The Siren Wars

Book Two: Darker Depths

Book Three: Beyond The Shores

Origins of the Siren Wars: Prequel Novella

The Jaded Duology

Book One: Jaded

Book Two: Risen

The Complete Series Boxset/Omnibus with exclusive epilogue
(Summer 2018)

The Golden Trilogy

Book One: Golden

Forged: A Golden Novella

Book Two: Locked

Book Three: Edge

The Complete Series Boxset/Omnibus with exclusive bonus novella, Tempered

The Legends Chronicles

Along Came A Spider: A Prequel Novelette

And They'll Come Home: A Prequel Novelette

The Revolution of Jack Frost (Coming November 2018)

Virtually Sleeping Beauty: A Novella Retelling

The Goose Girl and The Artificial: A Novella Retelling

THE SIREN WARS

War has hovered around the kingdom of Scylla for generations ever since the original sirens left the mer collection generations ago after nearly drowning the human prince. Over the years, select mermaids from the royal bloodline have been trained as spies to work for the reigning kings and queens, keeping the collection safe from sirens and humans.

Celena and her partner, Merrick, work covertly for the royals—not even her twin brother knows. When they discover the sirens have broken through the barriers the mer set up to keep the sirens out, Celena and her friends must race to the old kingdom of Metten to stop them from starting a war within their borders.

When she's dragged to the surface, Celena realizes that the war above the waters is as deadly as the one below the waves—and sacrificing herself may be the only way to protect her family.

The Siren Wars have only just begun.

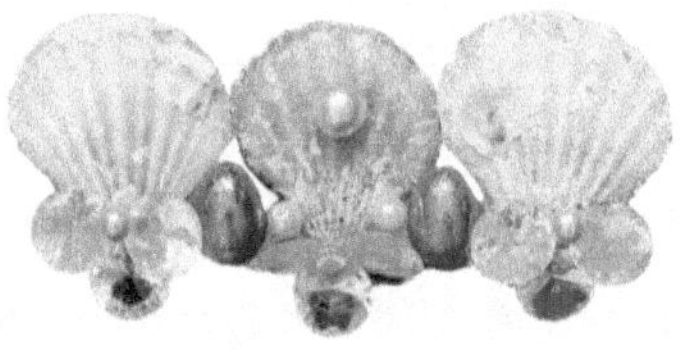

Get your copy at
sirenwarsinfo.kmrobinsonbooks.com

Read the first chapter on the next page!

THE SIREN WARS-CHAPTER 1

A WELL-PLACED ACCUSATION—EVEN A SMALL, insignificant one—has the power to change the tides and start a war.

This is something I've grown up learning.

My kind have always been careful with our words… we have to be. For the last one hundred years, we've had to fight against the actions of one mermaid. Well, to be fair, one mermaid, her mother, and a group of followers, but that's just semantics. For a hundred years before that, we had to be careful too—we had an agreement with the humans.

"Are you intentionally trying to look like that?" I ask, flicking my tail flirtatiously.

"Like what, Celena?" Merrick glances up from where

he's working on the sea floor against a rock, his brow low.

"Brooding," I reply.

His face lights up, realizing that he has been caught.

"Sorry, Len," he uses his pet name for me—no one else is allowed to call me that—as he moves the knife in his hands, cutting the rope.

He brushes his blue hair back with a smoldering grin before lifting himself off the sand, swimming over to me.

"Need a hand with that?"

"We're fine, Merrick," Caspian says. "Go back to not paying attention to the rest of us."

"I didn't miss *that* much," he mutters.

"*Sure*," Caspian replies.

Merrick gives him a mock-annoyed look, rolling his eyes as he grabs the net, helping us to untangle the rock.

"How did we get stuck on clean up duty?" Merrick asks, using his most charming voice as he sidles up next to me.

"We volunteered," I remind him.

"Mmm," he murmurs. "*You* volunteered. I just followed."

"Nothing new there, brother," Caspian teases loudly. "Always following my twin around no matter where she goes."

Caspian has *no idea* why Merrick and I spend so much time together.

"Shut up, Casp," Merrick chides, winking at me.

What neither of the boys knows is that I didn't volunteer just to help out—I'm on a mission.

"It amazes me how the humans are still so intent on capturing us," Caspian murmurs. "It's been a hundred years since Persephone ruined the alliance for us."

"Be fair, Casp—it wasn't *just* Persephone. Chantay was instrumental in all of this—most say she was the mastermind and her daughter just followed along."

My fingers work to cut away the net waving gently in the current. The knife in my hand is far more effective than the broken shells I sometimes resort to using for cutting up the instruments of death that fishermen leave in the ocean when they snag on something like coral or rocks.

"It's a shame we can't just sing this work away," Coralie swims over, attempting to carry a large, round ball. She barely manages to roll it across the sea floor.

"That's not the way sireny works, starfish," I correct her. "And stop playing with that canon ball."

My little sister pouts, looking up.

"I'm not playing with it, I'm trying to help," she mutters.

"We don't need to collect human things, just remove the dangerous ones," I remind her. Coralie has only been out to help us a few times, but I'd rather she stay at home —she's too young for me to be able to sneak off and run missions while she's with us, and Caspian will start to catch on if I dump her in his care all the time.

"It would still be easier if we could sing it away," she grumbles, running hair hands through her blonde hair.

"We are not sirens, Cor, and don't even suggest that," I snap. Caspian and Merrick stop to look at me. I try not to blush as I lower my voice. "We are not like that, Coralie. Sireny has been outlawed since great-great-grandmother Aila caught Persephone sirening the prince."

"We're better off," Caspian mumbles. "We don't need the humans to survive. They haven't been able to find us in a hundred years anyway, so who cares what stupid stunt Persephone and her mother pulled?"

"You mean *aside* from hundreds of dead humans, the mer population splitting, our entire kingdom having to leave our home and move here, and—*oh, yes*—the entire human race hunting us for a century?" I chide him.

"Settle down, children," Merrick chimes in, playfully trying to quell an impending argument.

This is why Caspian has never been informed of my extracurricular activities over the last few years. This is also why Merrick *has* been on most of my missions with me.

"Well, maybe we could train the sharks to move this stuff for us," Coralie suggests.

I certainly have my hands full with this one.

"Coralie, it's all we could do to train them to act as a barrier for Scylla, *for coral's sake.* It's not like they're pets—they don't have the ability to open things like an octopus does. They're there to eat—that's all."

"Well maybe grandma Aila should have come up with a better plan," Coralie mumbles.

"Aila saved us all, Cor," I eye her. "Show a little respect. She prevented Persephone from destroying the entire mer population. She even managed to bring Persephone in from the open seas."

I idolized my great-great-grandmother and aunts—they were heroes. Aila even saved the humans, though they didn't *deserve* her help one bit.

"Princess Kailania helped," Coralie persists. "So did Ebba. And Chantay went on to live and cause destruction for *years* before she died."

"Coralie," Merrick interrupts, flicking his hand to send a small seahorse toward her. "You understand the sirens terrorize the mer *and* the humans, right? Your ancestors did a great thing when they set up the shark barrier to prevent them from attacking us here in Scylla."

Coralie has always loved the stories of our great-great-grandmother and always wanted to visit the old kingdom, so she's just being stubborn because she doesn't want to work.

"I know," she sighs. My sister tries to suppress her

grin when the brown seahorse darts by her. "I just wish this were easier—or more fun."

"Tell you what," I smile, suddenly getting an idea. "Why don't you let Casp take you home and Merrick and I will finish up here. We're almost done anyway."

She cheers before my twin can protest. He grumbles, brushing back his hair.

"You two behave," he pretends to be serious, pointing at us. He wraps his arm protectively around our sister and guides her through the currents along the ocean floor.

When I turn back around, Merrick is working overtime to cut up the abandoned net. He nods for me to join him.

"I take it we have somewhere to be?" he asks casually.

"Yes."

"You weren't planning on taking me along, were you?" Merrick glances at me through his long, wavy bangs.

He caught me.

"It's not a big deal."

"Everything we do is a big deal, Celena. Every time we get near the shark barrier or swim up one of the reefs, it's a big deal."

"They wouldn't have trained us for this if they didn't want us to do it," I say, rolling my eyes at him.

"Just remember *which one of us* nearly swam into a

bloom of jellyfish last time we went out *alone*," he reminds me with a smirk.

"I only did that because you showed up and distracted me."

"You mispronounced *saved*." He grins wildly.

"Hardly, pretty boy."

We snap each rope on the net, making sure no mer or sea creature would get tangled in it. At least this one wasn't covered in barbs like the last one I found.

"I like your *iluse* today," Merrick adds, eyeing my chest covering. "Judging by those weapons you hid on it and called decorations, I'm guessing your little mission isn't as serene as you led me to believe."

Of course he'd notice the broken shells I hid in the netting and decor of my top—Merrick notices *everything*.

I slip my knife into the pouch tucked along my belt where it rests over my hips as my partner does the same. Belts were always traditionally worn by mermen a century ago to show power and prestige. The mermen would wear them specifically for special events or if they held a place of power. Now, most mer have a version they wear, especially when going to town or leaving the kingdom proper.

"So where are we going?" Merrick asks.

"This way," I reply, darting away.

I race around the seaweed gardens, swimming just

high enough that their wispy tips don't touch me as I glide over them. A sea turtle swims off to the left, not bothering to take notice of us.

"There's been word that the sirens have found a way in on the west side of the kingdom. I just want to check and make sure nothing has changed since we've last been there."

"Did they *ask* you to check?" Merrick challenges me.

"She doesn't have to," I snip, flicking my tail to propel me faster, leaving Merrick in a trail of bubbles.

"*She* the queen or *she* your mother?" He easily catches up to me, having a far more powerful tail than I do.

"Take your pick," I retort.

"It's rough being princess to the entire mer kingdom, isn't it?" Merrick mocks.

"I'm barely a princess," I remind him, darting around a school of fish. Merrick pulls away at the last second, barely missing them as I smirk.

"You descend from royalty. Just because your cousin holds the official crown, doesn't make you any less of a princess."

"I'm a warrior, Merrick. I hardly sit around the palace all day."

"Neither does your cousin," he points out as we slow our pace. "You all work for this kingdom. *You* just take it more seriously than the rest."

"Aila did."

"You don't have to do everything Princess Aila did," he counters. "And if you'll recall, she didn't set out to do any of that—it just happened.

"Next thing I know, you'll be swimming to the surface to meet some human prince." He rolls his eyes at me as he brings up Prince Jarek, the human Persephone tried to siren when she caused the war.

"I have no intention of befriending a human, thank you very much. That would be a stroke in the wrong direction for sure."

"Ah, but speaking of a stroke in the *right* direction, looks like our rides just arrived," Merrick calls, rushing forward. His hand darts out, catching hold of a dolphin.

He quickly reaches back, grabbing my hand as the creature pulls us forward. Once he pulls me to him, I catch my own ride.

The coral barrier stretches up high toward the surface of the ocean, protecting Scylla from intruders. The barrier blocks larger ships from entering most of the territory, protecting us from many of the humans' attempts to find us.

While their searches have slowed, it's very clear that they are not done looking for trophies to take home. A year ago, I found a book that had fallen to the ocean floor describing the most absurd ideas the humans had about mer. One page detailed our bone structure—which, in fact, they *do* know from cutting up our ancestors—while another page contained information about how we cry pearls and dissolve into foam when we have our hearts broken.

Humans are curious creatures who *clearly* haven't learned much in the last two centuries.

When we finally let go of the dolphins, Merrick and I examine the coral. Nothing looks out of place, though it's been months since I was last here. I only make it out to this side of the kingdom a few times a year, just to check on it. We have mermen standing watch at all times, but I like to see it for myself.

"What I don't understand is how the sirens have been getting in," Merrick murmurs. "We have all of these barriers in place—we're protected. How are they slipping in?"

"We've only seen evidence of a few so far—barely enough to warn the people."

"We've never officially found any inside Scylla, I know." Merrick sighs. "But *how* is this possible?"

The few sirens we've noticed have disappeared before we could bring them in for questioning—the mer have only seen them from a distance.

Rumors have spread like seaweed that the sirens have changed in appearance—long, hideous noses, scraggly hair, and sea serpent-like tails.

I know that can't be true based on the books I've found from the humans. Sirens still look just like the mer—because they still *are* mer. They just cultivated their wicked talents while the mer forced it out of our offspring.

Once, we all had the ability to sing a human into doing our bidding. Now, only sirens hold that dark magic. Instead, we avoid humans and their destruction, leaving us no need for the deadly songs sirens have the ability to sing.

True, Marcelline—*the defender of the sea*—originally sirened King Leon into creating an agreement with the mer, but that only lasted a century until Persephone ruined that promise of safety for us. Marcelline's great-great-granddaughter, Aila, tried desperately to save the agreement and repair our relationship with the humans, but today we find ourselves living deep under the sea, refusing to venture to the surface where we once used our voices to save humans on the rough ocean surface.

Now, we wouldn't surface to save a drowning fisherman or guide a ship safely through a storm for any price. We don't associate with the population trying to murder us.

"Can you feel that?" Merrick asks, holding his arms out to his side. "The tide is changing. Just beyond the coral reef, the temperature drops. It's not a terrible difference, but just enough to be noticeably cooler."

I pause, giving Merrick his moment. Truthfully, I can sense the difference as the water drifts around me.

"I still don't see anything different," I finally announce.

"I don't either." He frowns. "We should go. We'll come up with another idea."

Instead of turning around with him, I flip my tail, propelling myself toward the surface. A moment later, Merrick is by my side, grumbling.

Careful not to touch the coral to avoid damaging it, I peer over the top of it, looking out into the blue ocean. Seaweed waves against the current while small fish swim in and out of the grass.

A shadow passes over the sea floor, stealthily gliding over rocks, sand, and seahorses. I gasp.

"Get down," Merrick commands, pulling me down below the top of the coral. I struggled to get away.

"No," I protest, prying his fingers off my waist. "We need to see the ship."

Reluctantly, he swims us both back up to the edge.

The ship drops a net that silently slices through the water. Fish dart out of the way as the fishermen search for dinner—or a mer trophy to string up on their mast before taking them back to land to show their people.

We watch as the net drags through the ocean, something shiny sparkling from the ropes. Suddenly, a figure darts out from behind the coral on the ground. She races toward the net, swimming as quickly as she can.

"What is she doing?" Merrick whispers as the mermaid catches up to the net.

The mermaid suddenly changes course, propelling herself straight up to the middle of the net. She tries untangling the shiny object from the rope. When she can't free it, she struggles against it, pulling as hard as she can to rip the object free.

It's hard to see her from so far away as she thrusts her hands deeper into the net, frantically trying to retrieve the object. After a moment, her movements change as anger and frustration shift to panic.

"She's stuck," I murmur.

"Celena," Merrick quickly warns, looking at me. "We can't."

"We can't let them take her," I plead with him.

"She's a siren. King Gaspar made it very clear we aren't allowed to help them."

"King Gaspar has been dead for nearly a century," I protest. "Even so, he did everything in his power to try to keep us all together."

"You realize that only one of us gets forgiveness if we decide to become a rebel, right?" Merrick remarks, giving me a look before glancing at the mermaid. The net lifts toward the surface and his face falls.

"Merrick," I shout. My worry was in vain—Merrick was already swimming over the reef.

I flick my tail, racing forward to follow him as we rush toward the siren. No matter how hard we try, we'll never reach her in time.

The last thing I see is her red tail lifting out of the water, her wrist still tangled in the net as she screams. Merrick never slows, pushing to reach her.

"Merrick!" My shouts don't deter him. He doesn't stop until she's gone. My friend pauses in the water, floating in the bubbles that trailed off of the mermaid's thrashing tail.

"We have to go." His voice is dark when he turns back to me. I stare at the bottom of the boat, far closer than it should be. "Len, *we have to go.*"

As quickly as a dolphin, Merrick dives at me, knocking me out of my trance. He pushes me back, tail beating against the water to move us away from the boat and out of siren territory.

"Merrick, we can't leave her."

"Oh, yes, we can," he says as if it's not an option. "I wasn't joking about this grace thing—we crossed a line just now. As a royal, you might be given leniency, but I certainly will not."

"Our mothers worked together, Merrick—you'll be fine."

Something sparkles above us, reflecting off the water.

Red trickles down, slowly fading to where the sky meets the sea.

A firework—a celebration of a mermaid catch.

"Right now, they're tying that mermaid to the beams on their ship, Celena. I won't have them do that to you—we're leaving."

"Merrick, she's a mermaid. She's about to suffer the unthinkable. Maybe we can rescue her."

"You know that's been attempted before and hasn't worked," he argues. He's terrified for my safety and while I understand that, I can't just swim away.

"None of those mer know as much about humans as you and I do—we've studied them," I reply.

"From books. We've studied them *from books.*" He looks desperate, pleading with me to turn back.

"We have to," I whisper.

"Len," he whispers back. His fingers grip the shell necklace that rests on his chest. When he sighs, I know I've won.

He grabs my hand as we race after the boat. The water rushes against my ears, flooding my senses. We push harder, forcing ourselves beyond what any mer is normally capable of doing.

My hand slips to the knife on my hip. I fumble for it, unable to detach it as I swim toward the human boat—I doubt it would do any good, even if we *could* reach them.

"Stay below the surface," Merrick warns, grasping my hand tighter.

Bits of my pink hair float around me as we come to a sudden halt. We're far enough away from the boat that the men likely won't take notice of us, but close enough that I can see them trying to tie the thrashing mermaid to the mast of their ship. She struggles against them, trying to siren them into submission.

Her singing appears to be working as most of the men back away. Several untie her as she frantically sings. I'm mesmerized by her ability to control them.

"I didn't think that was possible," I murmur.

I know that we once all had the ability to control humans with our voices, but over the last century, that skill was taken away from us, trained out of our people until it no longer existed. To see sireny so strong was an incredible experience—I almost wish I could surface and listen to her song.

They pass her along the deck of the ship near the edge, close enough that we can see her moving. Not everyone is under her spell though—several men race toward her in anger.

The edge of the ship covers our view. Merrick holds me back. In my distraction, I had nearly surfaced to see the scene unfold.

"We can help her if she makes it into the water, but

Len, we have to be careful. Your mother will kill me if you get hurt."

"You're more scared of my mother than you are of the queen," I snap back.

When the mermaid crashes into the ocean, red plumes around her, mimicking the color of her tail.

Read the rest by grabbing your copy of The Siren Wars at sirenwarsinfo.kmrobinsonbooks.com

JADED: BOOK ONE OF THE JADED DUOLOGY

Her father failed in his mission to take control from the Commander, a defeat that has cost Jade her life. She will die as punishment. Now she belongs to the Commander's son—as his wife. Knowing his intent is to quietly kill her in revenge, Jade's every move is calculated to survive—until she learns her death ensures the safety of her father and her entire town.

Roan doesn't want to kill Jade, but once his family isolates her from her father and community, his only choice is to go through with the plan. Jade doesn't make it easy as she tries to sway him into falling for her. Each misstep makes him question his cause. Each moment makes every decision harder, but the Commander won't allow him to fail.

One chooses life. One chooses death. In the midst of the chaos, only one will succeed.

Now available!
Learn more about The Jaded Duology at
jadedinfo.kmrobinsonbooks.com

GOLDEN: BOOK ONE OF THE GOLDEN TRILOGY

Goldilocks was never naive. She was sent on a mission and Dov Baer is her new target.

When the girl with the golden hair betrays everyone, not even she has hope of surviving.

The stories say that Goldilocks was a naïve girl who wandered into a house one day. Those stories were wrong. She was never naïve. It was all a perfectly executed plan to get her into the Baers' group to destroy them.

Trained by her cousin, Lowell, and handler, Shadoe, Auluria's mission is to destroy the Baers by getting close to the youngest brother, Dov, his brother and sister-in-law and the leaders of the Baers' group.

When she realizes Dov isn't as evil as her cousin led her to believe, she must figure out how to play both sides or her deception will cause everyone in her world to burn.

If her allegiances are discovered, either side could destroy her...if the Society doesn't get her first.

Available now!
Learn more about The Golden Trilogy at
goldeninfo.kmrobinsonbooks.com

ALONG CAME A SPIDER: THE FIRST PREQUEL NOVELETTE TO THE LEGENDS CHRONICLES

Little Hacker Muffet
sat on her tuffet
destroying her cords and Way.
Along came a hacker named Spider,
who sat down beside her
and frightened his opponent away.

WHEN FET, ONE OF THE MOST SKILLED HACKERS IN THE Legends, discovers her best friend and leader of her group has been abducted and held for ransom, she must escape unnoticed and find Peep before it's too late.

When Spider, a new recruit training to join her hacker ring, slips out with her and claims to have a plan to save her friend, Fet is forced to bring him along. As she discovers he's not who he claims to be, she faces grave danger and learns just how deadly a spider bite can be.

Now available!
Learn more about The Legends Chronicles at
acasinfo.kmrobinsonbooks.com

VIRTUALLY SLEEPING BEAUTY

She may be doing battle in the virtual world, but in the real world, they can't wake her up...

All Rora wants is to help people as class president, give her time to local charities, and quietly earn her way to the top level of the virtual reality system that the entire country uses without anyone noticing she's the second best player in the game.

All Royce wants to do is level up as a knight inside the gaming system, slay dragons, and eventually play his way to controlling the palace as he takes the crown away from the reigning queen.

When his Aunt Perry calls him, hysterically screaming that her goddaughter, Rora, has been inside for more than the four hours the game allows, Royce rushes over to help.

Entering the game, Royce soon discovers that Rora is trapped inside the system after an encounter with an evil magician who can change forms inside the game and control the virtual world. If he and his friend can't help her beat the game, she might not be able to wake up in the real world at all.

When virtual knights and princesses meet to slay dragons and defeat evil rulers, there's nothing stopping them from suffering real-world consequences too.

To wake her up, he must enter the game and help her beat it.

Now available!
Learn more about Virtually Sleeping Beauty at
vsbinfo.kmrobinsonbooks.com